I0670679

sad
sad
boy

stone hares

The hares now have their winter coats on. In the morning, as you cut through the woods to drop the boy at nursery, it's like the stones are moving. The hares are moving around. Stones don't move. You want to tell someone.

truck

Sad boy goes online. He checks his email. He checks some baseball results. He checks Twitter. Some drama is unfolding in a group chat. Johnny Utah is trolling people with edgy alt-right shit. Some feather-wearing kid is inflamed by one sad boy or another. It's all gone a little wrong. One member of the group has decided that their gender is now a truck. Yes, a truck, like a vehicle. Sad boy just wants to get along with people and stop feeling so lonely. He decides to log off and goes for a walk.

sad sad boy

michael o'brien

copyright © michael o'brien, 2022
printed in the usa
published by back patio press
first edition, 2022
all rights reserved.

Design by zac smith
typeset in young and helvetica

isbn: 978-1-7332757-9-8

this is all fiction. names, characters, business, events and incidents are the products of the author's imagination. any resemblance to actual people, places, or events is purely coincidental.

some of the following have previously appeared, in slightly altered form, online: "feeling like shit," "sack of meat," and "the earth is flat first" *in back patio press*; "my son doesn't think" and "the female ecuadorian basketball team" in *nauseated drive*; "3am," "momma's shells," "blueberry," and "portrait" in *otoliths*; "cheese" and "emilio and the frog" in *expat*; "ugly sad boy," "walk-in," "sad art boy", "it is late at night, again," and "summer moths" in *cavity magazine*; "tape face gets a new book," "sad boy and his pen," and "the wall" in *misery tourism*; "you won't hear a friend out of me," "easter hymnal," and "you googled banana bread recipe" in *synchronised chaos*. thank you to the editors.

sad sad

boy

recycling

Watching a couple recycling a child looks on approvingly. Sorta smug and stupid. You feel a warmth growing inside. What a wholesome world. We have bread, democracy and birds. The child looks at you. A question sparkles in his eyes. Before he has a chance to ask the question you hit him really hard with a book about Central American beetles.

feeling like shit in the happiest place on earth

I scheduled an interview with the post office but I couldn't make it due to the fact I'm finding it hard to breath. Likely story. Anyway, I'm at the doctors now – more accurately I'm in a queue to see a receptionist. My number comes up. She gives me a torturous time. I am sweating and dying. Wonderful. On one side of her cubicle are two pictures of cats. One is smiling in a photoshop kinda way. The other is a cat in a more natural pose. Seems like it might be her cat. Maybe her cat that died. I don't really know.

She thumps away at her keyboard. She thumps away at me with questions. All I say is here is my health card. I am sick. Let me see a doctor, please. On the other cubicle wall is a picture of a woodpecker in a lovely pastoral setting feeding its young. I get a sense that the receptionist is not into woodpeckers. I get through the questions and forms. I see a nurse first and she takes bloods and that kind of thing. Finally get to see the doctor. He is thorough, competent and polite. A good boy. He doesn't waste words and tells me little. He sends me for more bloods and a throat swab. I head back to my flat. At the flat I take a nap. Wake up

he hates himself and wants to go make tyres

He announces he is quitting poetry and going to make car tires instead. No one replies or likes the tweet. He feels sad. Like, useless. He desires to have suicidal thoughts so he can just kill himself but he just can't be suicidal. He hates himself so much. He envies the attention cancelled celebrities get. He'd loved to be popular enough that people would care about how much of a piece of shit he is. He'd do anything to feel genuine hatred. Anything. He stops for a moment of drama. He takes out a notebook and starts drawing different car tyres.

the library

Sad boy goes to the library. He wants to get some art books. In the library a librarian is berating a homeless man. Sad boy thinks it's sad the way the homeless man is being treated. He doesn't say anything although he's seen that librarian before. That librarian came to him in a dream. It was sad. He leaves the library without any books.

and drink coffee. I wait for blood results. I hear the woodpecker. I think he is smacking against the lampposts again. It's also raining.

momma's shells

Your mother wanted shells. You shot at the toy poodle. The dog turned its head towards you and then back to its original position and then walked off. You put your hands in your pockets. You awkwardly pretended to search for something. After a short while you wondered where the dog went.

sad art boy

Your exhibition wasn't going well at all. It had been open all week. Only two people came into the gallery. One wanted to use the toilet – you lied and said there was no toilet. The other was lost – you said nothing to them. You hung your head to hide your shame and waited for them to leave. It took them fifteen seconds to leave. You counted. You count good.

it is late at night, again

Someone drives past. They are going fast. You are sure someone shouts your name from the speeding vehicle. You try to shout your name back at them. But you fumble over the second syllable. You feel foolish and go home alone again.

rare birds

How many rare birds have appeared when you were not looking? You are the same age as Laura Dern. but you did not star in Jurassic Park. A pied flycatcher lands in front of you. It is not a rare bird. But it is beautiful.

3am

It is 3AM. You are awake. You want to sleep but something has crafted a barbed mountain out of your skull. Oh. You think about your two favourite conspiracy theories that involve Tupac and cryptids. You think about eating something even though you are not hungry. You process the night colours of the curtains, carpet, rug and coach. The smell of things, too.

You go to lie down. You put your phone on charge beside the bed. Ok. You want to say something to make sure your voice still works. Who will pick cotton on the far side of the moon? The phone's light fades out.

you won't hear a friend out of me

Summer ends. You buy a bag of carrots. You take the bag of carrots home. You open a bag of carrots.

Hey, is anyone one in there?
Nothing. Nothing in the bag of carrots but the quietness of carrots.
You ask again but louder.

easter hymnal

how to poison eggs:

Pacific ocean. Joauquin phoenix. Tulips. Rimbaud. Fish. Dead editors. Birds of Suriname. Soldiers playing with beetles. When they make a movie about you, you disappear. Baking competitions. A river with no name. Things that bother you. Alphabet spaghetti. The sound of an approaching train. Rivers that begin with the letter q. Kurt Cobain's last dream. Too long in the sun. Mary Magdalene's 1991 donruss rookie card. Jay feathers. Virtue signaling. Cool breeze. Napoli. Scuffed knees. Paint factory. Street signs facing the wrong way.

you googled banana bread recipe

and now it is baseball season again.

your hair is still your hair.
you trimmed it yesterday.
but it is still yours.
like the banana bread you baked yesterday.

the snow has started to shift.
and the roads are wet from melting ice
not rain

you found the recipe
after you googled banana bread recipe

and now it is baseball season again.

sad song

Pentagons cool in autumnal remembrance. Sad songs of a heavyweight's illness. Barren cold up high clouds lose their minds and become sad like the rest of us. The tollbooth just a name for wanderers to ponder on a distant map. So it is. A cat taking a piss.

summer moths

That summer you decided to take two months off. Most of the day you sat around reading the books – one of two things your father left in his will. In the evenings, an hour before twilight, you took a walk along the river Moy. The river wound around the fields and was shaded by large willows. These trees provided a perfect habitat for the surrounding wildlife. There was an abundance of wildlife there from birds to insects. And with the insects the second thing your father left you came in. He had left a moth trap. At first you thought about selling it online, but even though you weren't that close, it seemed cruel. So that summer you read a few Reddit posts on how to use it and started a new twilight hobby. Most people recommend that you set the trap before dusk and check it in the morning. You've never done mornings so you checked the trap in the evening. The moths were beautiful in the fading light. You never bothered learning their names or identifying them. You just took them out of the trap and let them sit on your hand admiring their beauty before they took off into the abounding night sky.

he didn't notice

You looked good tonight
Is that all you have to say?

I felt ashamed at his abruptness. His rudeness. I examined my shoes. I saw creases in the plastic. I saw dust in little spots like an orchid rosette. With this shame I wanted to disappear but I knew it wasn't an option. I decided I wanted my feet to become mushrooms. As the thought took root in my brain it lost control. I really wanted my feet to become mushrooms. And I thought about it real hard and sure enough they did.

My boyfriend was so absorbed in his hatred for me he didn't notice. We got into the taxi when it came and went home. All the while my feet were bright red toadstools. *Wow,* I thought to myself. *They are two cool looking mushrooms.*

let's horse sometime

I lived that horse in your poem.
I mean, I was that horse.
I mean, that mood your poem created – I lived it.
Ok. Yes, let's meet in the horse some time.
Let's meet in a horse some time.

ugly sad boy

The bathroom light is harsh. You feel ugly. You notice ugly things. Deformity upon deformity. Rock on rock. Bird poop on bird poop. You decide to fix your eyebrows. You comb them with a large lady's hairbrush. You like how it feels and looks. The oversized brush covers most of your face. Deciding you want the brush to stay in front of your face you look for some kind of adhesive. You find that stuff that keeps dentures in place and start applying it liberally from your chin to your hair line.

walk-in

In the woods you see some of last year's fallen acorns. You start eating them. You eat them because you saw a post on Reddit highlighting how they can kill your soul. You want your soul to die. You want a new soul. You want to be a better person. You keep eating acorns.

cheese

You pick the cheese up. You become cheese. You pick the cheese up. You put the cheese down. You become cheese. You put down the cheese.

The cheese, now you, thinks a soft nebulous thought. And now, this thought, the cripples' crutch hollowed. And now, this thought, the agency of summer horses.

it is raining. it is easter

Father is grieving the loss of his parents. They died almost 15 years ago. It is raining today. The weather is cool today. It is Easter today. He picks up a stone on Easter. He picks up a stone today. He picks up some paper and makes two little figures and pretends they are his parents. He breastfeeds from his paper mother. Paper father does nothing but stand there like all paper dads do. Although the milk is nothing but liquid paper, it is sweet and nourishing.

vegetables for the sad boy

Sad boy buys some seeds. He plants them good – with fertiliser and all that nice stuff. He believes he has planted tomatoes. But they are actually something much much different. They are actually a rare plant that increases and eventually doubles one's student debt. He finds this out much too late. And now he has crippling debt and no tomatoes.

emilio sad sad boy tries to break horses

You try to google how to break horses but your search is mysteriously redirected to results regarding *The Breakfast Club. The Breakfast Club*, you ask no one. No one is ever around. *Fuck this movie*, you say to the thousand horses in your mother's house racing by the windows. They are brown on top and white on the bottom. They are beautiful. They look good.

the female Ecuadorian basketball team

What took you so long?
An Ecuadorian basketball team.

I handed him the bag of groceries. He started putting the items where they should be when they are not in a shop and we continued talking.

What?
I mean the Female Ecuadorian basketball team.
How'd you know they were from Ecuador?

He closed the cupboard a little too hard. It made a noise that was a little too loud.

They had on tracksuits with a basketball logo that had Ecuador written around it.
Yep. That sounds like Ecuadorians and basketball players. You can never be too sure though. Were they tall?
A little above average height but they were quite muscular.
What did they buy?

He put the last of the items away. Folded the bag neatly and put it in its designated place. And then he put himself in his designated place. And I continued.

Mostly apples. Some things I couldn't see.
Which colour?
Red.

the frog and the sad boy

Sad boy goes to a pond. A frog sits there. The frog tells him to cut his fingers off. *No,* says sad boy, *I'm gonna start a literary website that seems like it is highlighting others' work but all the while boosts my own profile.* The frog says, *I think you should cut your fucking fingers off, bro.*

tape face gets a new book

Sad boy thinks that all poems are about him. His mind twitches. He's over-caffeinated and over-tired. He's read the new book he got. It's a poetry book. It's about barns. He thinks about barns for a while. He thinks about the one where his dad keeps the wood and turf for the winter. Then he thinks about rivers. And then rivers that run by barns. And then back to how much he hates himself.

sad boy and his pen

Sad boy buys a vintage fountain pen on ebay. He spends a whole welfare check on it. It arrives on a Wednesday. He opens the package. *Wow,* he says. His mind flits between the new pen and the people lurking in a Twitter group chat he's in. Wow, what a great pen. He then decides it's time to use the pen. He spits on the pen. He drops his pants and inserts it in his anus. For a second the lurkers come back to him and then he starts stroking his cock till he comes. He leaves the pen in his anus and logs on to Twitter.

the wall

She ends the call. She puts the phone in her inside pocket and walks back to her beige car and her waiting partner. As she gets within spitting distance of the car she smiles at the partner but he doesn't notice as he is reading a food wrapper. A look weighted equally in boredom and studiousness covers his face. Just as she is less than a meter away from the car the wall beside it disappears and so does she. The whole vanishing act takes less than a second. The wall eventually returns but she doesn't.

in the stillness of summer

I rushed back after visiting hours. I needed definitive answers. I needed to know why he did it. His room had been untouched. His bed unmade. His laptop closed. His wardrobe closed. Clothes and bits of this and that strewn everywhere. The laptop would be an obvious place to start but I decided to look at that last because it would probably be password protected. I looked under his pillows. Under the bed. Little nooks and crannies. Under bits and bobs. Nothing of significance. And then I opened his wardrobe. It was the only neat place in the whole house, let alone room. A stack of old music magazines – *The Source, NME, Mojo*. His clothes hanging lifeless. His hats. And then where the shoes should have been a little man – maybe half a foot tall – stood there, petrified, staring at me. He was naked and looked rather gnome-like. Silently we looked at each other, him scared, me dumb. I closed the door and pretended I hadn't seen anything. *I will deal with this shit later,* I thought.

I went downstairs. Then Colin walked in. He was carrying Hazel's dog Max. They were both covered in blood.

What happened?
Max got shot by a spaceship
A spaceship?
A spaceship

The dog whined

We should call a doctor
Yeah, or a vet.

Colin was covered in Max's blood and was also carrying Max so I called the vet. I thought to myself, *Wow it's a good thing I remembered a random vet's number.* As the phone rang out I thought about the suicide and the little man in the cupboard and Max being shot by a spaceship and started to feel really fucking sad.

bmx track in the woods

It is night and you feel sad again. You are alone in your room. You are listening to music on headphones. You open your notebook. You sketch a bmx track surrounded by tall trees. Eventually your pencil becomes dull and you stop and notice your sadness again.

my better-looking ugly twin

In my third year of high school a boy transferred from South Africa. He walked into the classroom. We were silent with curiosity. As he looked up and towards the teacher, Alex bellowed, *O'Brien, is that your twin?* A half second of silence and then the boy blushing looked up and everyone burst out laughing. Oh my God. Shock stock phrases. An agreement rumbled through the room. I felt sorry for my sad ugly twin who was slightly better looking than me because he had a nice haircut and good posture. I never talked to him once in the next two years of high school.

Portrait

you wanted to be a cheese monger
but your willy is too small

you wanted to be a twenty-foot horse
but they aren't that big

you bought every wu tang affiliate album
but ignored killarmy

you took a photo of a bridge
where the mothman appeared
on the day you were born
nice
it got three hundred retweets when you posted it on
twitter the following week
also nice

you bought a pear from the shop
and looked at the natural colours
and you were reminded of your skin
and its freckles in the summer

danny devito

Your heart is the size of Danny Devito. Your heart is
five feet tall and all together you are six feet tall. Your
legs are half a foot in length the same as your head.
You have no arms. You are mostly heart. You poop
out of the bottom of your heart. You make breakfast in
a clumsy, all-heart way. Most people find it endearing.
You find it difficult. You find life challenging and
generally unpleasant.

in a taxi

The suspension or something is off. The motion starts to make you feel sick. You run an inventory of things to distract yourself so you don't vomit. You think of the smell of salt. This works a little. You look up at the sun where it always is at this time of the day.

sack of meat netflix special

The producer, the camera man and the sound guy start to shove the meat into a see-through bag. The meat is unidentifiable – none of them know which animal or what part of the animal it came from. They don't discuss this. The sound guy picks up his sound equipment. The camera man goes to his camera. The producer picks up the sack of meat and props it on a chair behind a desk in front of the camera. The producer makes sure he is out of shot and starts to prod the sack of meat with a stick. It squelches and makes other sack of meat noises. They non-verbally decide to put a grey suit on the sack of meat. The producer starts the prodding routine again. Squelch. Sack of meat noises. Five minutes pass. Then fifteen. Another fifteen. And then words start to come out of the sack of meat. All three of them smile reassuringly. The prodding continues. And the words continue.

wanking goalkeepers

Some goalkeepers play soccer and kick goalposts for good luck.

Some goalkeepers play hockey and they masturbate every second day.

There are goalkeepers in other sports, too. Some of them probably collect rare rocks from the valley floor. Blue rocks. Blue rocks. And more blue rocks that sometimes look purple in certain types of light.

department store cargo pants

There's no way to shake this off. It may be an eyelash in an eye, as you put it. It may be the young brains plastered all over the wall. His piss covered pants. His muddy boots. It's more. I don't know. They know I won't do anything; they know I am ideologically opposed to killing myself. But I drink too much. And they know I drink too much. And we know all bets are off when most of us are drunk. Right?

the saucepan

This saucepan has a unique feature. Its handle is hollow but not closed in. This is not remarkable or even interesting. But sometimes when you take it out of the dishwasher, water that has gathered in the hollow unsealed handle splashes all over you.

expression

You put the tv on. The news comes on with the tv. You sit down. There is big news on the news on the tv. But first the government insists on your daily expressions. Today is Saturday. On Saturdays you must express yourself by first lighting a sea breeze scented Yankee candle and then dying of a virus. You woke up in a rebellious mood this morning so you decide to die of a virus first. But, just in case, you look around to make sure no one is watching.

a missing cat – the reward for any information is a signed picture of jodie foster

Yo, bro, I'm a missing cat. All your cats were eaten by werewolves. I'm a missing cat. I was eaten by werewolves.

buying a knife and pencil

One night as you are getting ready for bed you notice something similar to sadness. You're not sure what to do. You toss and turn all night. In the morning, feeling like shit, you decide to go treat yourself. You buy a knife. It is a nice knife – humble in its size and decoration. Afterwards you buy a pencil. It is a nice pencil. You go to the nice coffee place. You order a nice coffee. You take a nice serviette, too. You notice it is better quality than the toilet paper you regularly buy. Your toilet paper is normally white like all toilet paper and this serviette is yellow and has an anthropomorphic coffee cup on it. A unique form of Hell – being a sentient coffee cup that is.

You sit down and drink the coffee. On the yellow serviette you start a list of things to do with your knife. You write: *cut some fruits; show it to some girls to impress them; clean it.*

big fucking mall, bro

You go to this new mall that is marketed as the biggest mall in the Nordics. Ok. In the mall something is off. But you can't say what. They have all the right shops for clothes. All the right fast food chains for food. The right temperature. The right lights. Even a little place to put your dog as you go and consume. But still something is off. And then as you decide to go eat another chicken teriyaki sub you feel a stabbing sensation all over your body. You check your arms. Your legs. But nothing. Nothing visible. You race home quickly. And then you vomit for seven days and nights and then nothing else happens. And that's all. And then you go back to the mall.

the big dress

The dress just kept growing. *What kind of material is this*, he asked desperately skyward. And then the dress ate him. The last thing he noticed was a warm summer breeze and the smell of flowering mint. And the dress just kept growing until it was the only thing in the universe.

ed Norton

Tonight you feel sad again. You sit on a river bank. You think about your first love. He was a juggalo named Ed Norton.

I wwanted milk

I wwanted milk.
But this is pineapple.
That's what I'm saying.
But this is pineapple.

it's not a case of human's wanting change. it's more a case of our inability to change.

Like lowering the music enough to hear the cooling fan on a beat-up laptop. Nice. We're all very sad and tired. Nice.

january eggs and eggs in general

On the 9th of January the doctor told him the cause of the anaphylactic shock.

eggs?
it's a lot more common than you think, sir.
but how can an egg do that to him?

He pointed at his son in an equally dramatic and sincere gesture. He felt like he was in a HBO tv show. He thought fleetingly of the depiction of women in FBI crime dramas.

That night he drove around looking for chicken coops. On the outskirts of town he found a cooperative town farm behind a brewery with some generic name and logo with birds and flowers and stuff. Anyway, he went into the chicken coop and wrote obscenities like, *fuck off* and *chickens are arseholes* on the eggs. This made him feel good. That night he went home and slept real good. Deep and dreamless.

The next night he decided to do the same thing. *Fuck chickens*, he said to no one in particular as his nice car pulled out of his nice driveway. *Fuck chickens, am I right?* He went to the next town over, where they had a smaller cooperative town farm that also had a smaller chicken coop. He went by the lettuce. He went by the spuds. He went by the Japanese brassica that was somehow thriving in this climate. And arrived at the coop. He bent down and went in. He kicked a chicken or two. And then went for the eggs. He moved the hay and poked and then he felt something cold. *The fuck is this,* he asked the aggrieved chickens. They didn't answer. He shone the light down and focused on what revealed itself to be a dragon fruit. He picked it up. It was frozen solid – a cold hard mass in his hands. Beneath it he noticed a tiny mother and child that started to scream as his eyes focused on them.

blueberry was a sad boy from the past

The year was 1887. I was in one of the new schools in Arizona. It was a regular school for the time where kids mostly did normal kid things. Then came along a story about Blueberry. One week, just as spring was getting warmer, rumours abound about a boy that liked to eat dog poop. Me and my gang were walking home from school one day when we spied Blueberry up ahead.

Hey Blueberry! We shouted.
He stopped, looked around and said, *What?*
We hear you eat dog shit! Billy the youngest of our gang shouted.
Yeah. What about it?

We were dumbfounded. None of us knew what to say. I looked off into the distance – I read somewhere that's what intelligent people do. I saw a hawk in the distance. And that's when I knew what to say.

Why you eat it? I asked in a presocratic tone.
Because it tastes good.

how to make a mantis

A mantis watches a young man. The young man is carrying a bottle of Tullamore dew. The mantis is in a transparent plastic box. The young man gets into a car. The car is both transparent and not – it is made of glass and metal. The mantis is in a pet shop window. The car drives away.

Later that evening the mantis watches a true crime documentary on Netflix. He feels a number of things but mostly feels sad because he has nobody to hold hands with. He farts and the last thing he thinks about before falling asleep is if he should have another beer.

my son doesn't think i'm a goat

Sometimes, when my son sees another man, he shouts *Daddy*. Daddy is his word for me and men in general. It is the same way with Mommy and women in general.

When he sees a goat, he makes a goat-like noise. When he does this I often ruffle his blonde locks just to let him know I am happy that he knows the difference between me and a goat.

meditation school for the sad boys

Sad boy went to a meditation school to learn magic and shapeshifting. He signed up for a whole year of daily classes and worked very hard. He was a sad boy but he was also a good boy – most sad boys are also good boys and are never lazy.

After the year was up he decided he'd test out his powers for real. Sad boy stood there and said the magic words he had learned. He felt proud of his hard work and good about the words. His spell was to become the morning – a perpetual state of being the morning. Bird song. Sunrise. Dew. All that good shit. But as the last syllable left his lips everything fell apart and he became a blade of grass.

What the sad boy was unaware of was that his meditation teacher was a phony. It is always hard to tell these things. The teacher looked the part – he had a robe, a moustache and a bell. He seemed legit. But sometimes dog poop in a tortilla wrap is not a burrito – it's just poopy poop.

So sad boy was now a blade of grass – which is neither sad, good nor happy. As a blade of grass, a dog visited him every day and pooped and peed on him. All summer long this continued. Dear God. And when it became cold and the first frosts arrived over the course of a week the sad boy, now a blade of grass, died a painful lonely frozen death.

michael o'brien is the author of numerous collections. his work has been published widely in print and on the internet and has been translated into other languages. he tweets at @mobrien222

www.ingramcontent.com/pod-product-compliance
Lightning Source LLC
Chambersburg PA
CBHW050906180626
46814CB00007B/2925